D0443270

PORTRAITS
of LITTLE WOMEN

A Gift
for Meg

Don't miss any of the
Portraits of Little Women

PORTRAITS
of LITTLE WOMEN

A Gift
for Meg

Susan Beth Pfeffer

DELACORTE PRESS

Published by
Delacorte Press
a division of Random House, Inc.
1540 Broadway
New York, New York 10036

Library of Congress Cataloging-in-Publication Data

Cataloging-in-publication data is
available from the Library of Congress.

ISBN: 0-385-32670-X

The text of this book is set in 13-point Cochin.

Book design by Patrice Sheridan
Cover art © 1999 by Lori Earley
Text art © 1999 by Marcy Ramsey
Activities art © 1999 by Laura Maestro

Manufactured in the United States of America

July 1999

10 9 8 7 6 5 4 3 2 1

BVG

TO BILL, MARCI, SARA, AND ALICE HANNERS

CONTENTS

PORTRAITS
of LITTLE WOMEN

*A Gift
for Meg*

CHAPTER 1

"Now, girls," Marmee said as she straightened Jo's collar and Beth's pinafore. "Be sure to listen politely to all of Aunt March's stories. Travel is very educational, and I'm sure there's a lot we can learn from what Aunt March will tell us."

Meg sighed. Aunt March was back from an extended trip to Europe, and whenever she returned from such a trip, she was full of stories for Father, Marmee, Meg, and her sisters.

Meg knew that Jo, who usually avoided Aunt March, always enjoyed the stories, probably because Jo yearned to travel as well. The stories allowed her to imagine that she was seeing all those grand sights herself.

Taking a quick look at Beth, Meg doubted that Beth found Aunt March anything other than terrifying. But Beth was too sweet to make a fuss. She listened to Aunt March and at least managed to seem entertained.

Amy, Meg's youngest sister, loved to hear anything about society. Since Aunt March stayed at the best hotels and occasionally met dukes and earls, Meg knew Amy was quite thrilled to listen to Aunt March ramble on.

As for Marmee, Meg was aware that her mother often found Aunt March tedious, but Marmee also loved new knowledge and appreciated learning all that Aunt March had to teach them about European cities and their famous sights.

That left only Meg, since Father was away that afternoon at a meeting. And only Meg wanted to be someplace, anyplace, else, rather than have to endure another of Aunt March's reminiscences.

Meg supposed someday she might travel,

and no doubt would on her honeymoon trip. But if her husband, whoever he might turn out to be, had no money for fancy trips, that was fine with Meg too. She wanted nothing more than a little cottage filled with happy children. If she could be half as contented as Marmee, Meg knew she'd be a lucky woman indeed.

Meg laughed at herself. How silly to be thinking about such a far-off life. She was only ten years old.

"You can laugh?" Jo asked. "With Aunt March on her way?"

"Jo," Marmee said. "Meg, what did you find so funny?"

"It was nothing, Marmee," Meg said. She knew her sisters wouldn't laugh at her if she told them what she'd been thinking about, but still, it was a private thought and not one she cared to share. Jo had no such fantasies about husbands and babies. Her dreams were far grander. Beth craved only the quiet of her daily life, and Amy daydreamed of nothing less than a duke of her own.

Only Meg seemed to want just what her

mother had: a happy marriage to a wonderful, loving husband, and four healthy children. Not that Meg particularly wanted her children to have the same natures as her sisters. And that thought made her laugh out loud again.

"Whatever the joke is, I wish you'd share it with us," Jo grumbled. "I can always use some cheering up when Aunt March is about to pay a call."

"I'll tell you later," Meg promised. She knew Jo would have forgotten the incident by the time they went to bed that night. Jo always had her mind on a hundred different things, and Meg's unexplained laughter wouldn't linger in her thoughts very long.

"Hush, girls," Marmee said. "Here's Aunt March's carriage now. Behave yourselves. Meg, dearest, you look lovely. But do try not to laugh when Aunt March comes in."

At first Meg thought Marmee was scolding her. But then she saw the laughter in her mother's eyes. "I'll barely smile," she said, and Marmee burst out laughing herself.

"My, this is a happy household," Aunt

March said as she entered the house. "When finances are strained, I suppose cheerfulness goes a long way."

"That it does," Marmee said, ignoring Aunt March's reminder of their modest means and kissing the older woman on the cheek. Meg and her sisters all kissed Aunt March too.

"The waters seem to have done wonders for you," Marmee said as she led them to the parlor. "You look quite rejuvenated, Aunt March."

"I admit, I had an excellent time on my travels," Aunt March said. "My companions were pleasant throughout, and I saw many different and unusual sights."

"Do tell us about them," said Jo. She sat by Aunt March's feet and looked up beseechingly. Meg stifled another giggle. It was so strange to see Jo actually eager to hear Aunt March's stories.

"Yes, please, tell us," Amy said. "Did you meet any dukes on this trip, Aunt March? I do love it when you meet dukes."

"I met one duke, two earls, and a count,"

Aunt March told her. "As well as duchesses, ladies, and countesses, of course. Not that any of those people are our betters. Aristocracy has no meaning for true American patriots."

"I know," Amy said. "But I would so love to meet a real duke."

"I'm sure you will someday," Aunt March said. "The one I met on this trip truly was a gentleman."

Meg tried to imagine herself marrying a duke. Then she'd be the Duchess Meg. The very idea made her want to laugh out loud, so she bit down hard on her tongue.

Catching a glimpse of Marmee, Meg realized that her mother was looking at her, obviously concerned about her behavior. This was unusual because Meg was the one in the family who tried to keep the others from misbehaving. Meg prided herself on her manners and knew Marmee approved of her ways. Marmee was a true lady, and it was often said that you could tell a lady by her manners.

But could you tell a duchess by hers? Meg

wondered, and she came so close to laughing that she had to bite her lip and stamp on her left foot with her right. Aunt March's visits could be so difficult!

"Meg, why don't you go to the kitchen and see if Hannah needs help with the tea?" Marmee suggested.

"Yes, Marmee," Meg said, rising rapidly from her chair. Her left foot positively throbbed, and Meg doubted she'd ever laugh again. Still, getting away from Aunt March was a good idea.

"No, Margaret, stay where you are," Aunt March said. "I brought you something from my European travels."

"Something for me?" Meg asked.

"I believe that's what I just said," Aunt March declared.

Meg sat back down. Aunt March wasn't one for giving gifts, and a present from Europe could be a true treasure.

"As you know from my letters, I spent much of my time in Brussels," Aunt March said. "I was quite favorably impressed with the Belgians. They seemed hardworking. And they make the most beautiful lace."

"I've heard of Belgian lace," Marmee said. "It's supposed to be lovely."

"That it is," said Aunt March. "Naturally, I brought some home for myself. But I purchased a piece for Margaret as well. I thought she might wish to save it for her wedding day."

"Might I look at it now?" Meg asked. She'd never been given such a special gift.

"I brought it with me," Aunt March said. She opened her carpetbag and took out a well-wrapped package, which she handed to Meg.

Meg opened the package carefully and removed the piece of lace. It was very long, Meg guessed five feet or longer, and the lace was delicate, with a lovely, intricate pattern.

"Oh, Aunt March," she cried. "It's so beautiful!" She ran over to her great-aunt and gave her a heartfelt kiss.

"You're a child now, but soon enough you'll be a grown woman," said Aunt March. "And

you'll want lovely things for your wedding. Now take care of this lace, Margaret. It's not a toy for you to play with."

"I'll cherish it, Aunt March," Meg said. "I promise." And that was a promise she intended to keep.

CHAPTER 2

As Aunt March spoke in detail of every European city she'd visited, and of every person she'd met, Meg could think of nothing but the lace. She couldn't get over the fact that Aunt March had thought about her even once on her journey, and that her thoughts had been of Meg's wedding day. Meg had never seen anything as lovely as the lace. She longed to examine it closely, memorize its pattern, and stand in front of a mirror to look at herself draped in it. Would she use it for her wedding veil? Or would it become part of her wedding gown?

Marmee would surely have several suggestions. Meg pictured herself and Marmee gazing at the lace for years to come, trying to decide how best to use it. And then, on Meg's wedding day . . .

But just as she imagined herself walking down the aisle, Father escorting her proudly, Aunt March harrumphed her farewells.

Meg raced over to her. "Thank you again, Aunt March," she said. "I shall cherish the lace forever."

Aunt March stared at her. Meg tried to think what else she was supposed to say.

"I don't know if I'll be here for your wedding day," Aunt March began.

"Why?" Amy asked. "Surely you wouldn't be in Europe on such an important occasion?"

Aunt March stared at Amy, then laughed. Amy was the only one of them who had a way of making Aunt March laugh.

"Out of the mouths of babes," Aunt March said. "What I meant was, I'm an old woman and I might have passed away by the time Margaret is married."

"Aunt March, you're in the best of health," Marmee said. "I'm sure you'll be with us for the weddings of all my daughters."

"It is not for us to foretell the future," Aunt March said. "Margaret, I trust wherever I may be on your wedding day, the lace will have special memories for you."

That was what Aunt March wanted! Meg would have kicked herself for not realizing it immediately, except that her foot still hurt. "The lace is lovely," she said. "What I will cherish most about it is your thoughtfulness, Aunt March."

This time Aunt March nodded. "You are a good girl, Margaret. I trust you will make a good match. One of you girls must, and it will be so much easier for the others, if you, as eldest, set a fine example. Now I must be going. Good-bye to you all."

Marmee and the girls kissed Aunt March. Meg could feel their collective relief as Aunt March's carriage began its drive back to her home.

"Let me see the lace," Jo demanded.

"Yes, Meg, show it to all of us," Amy said.

"I should love to see it as well," Beth said.

"Marmee, may I?" Meg asked.

Marmee smiled. "We should all be unhappy if you didn't," she said. "But handle it carefully. Such fine lace is delicate. I suspect Aunt March will inquire after it on a regular basis for years to come."

Meg unwrapped the package for a second time and carefully lifted out the lace. It was truly exquisite.

"I've never seen anything so wonderful," Beth said. "Oh, Meg, what a beautiful bride you'll make."

"It's perfect," Amy declared. "Put it on, Meg. Drape it around yourself so we can see what you'll look like when you get married."

Meg looked at Marmee, who nodded. Meg lifted the lace and with the utmost care draped it around her head.

"You look like a duchess," Amy said.

"No," Beth said. "A princess."

"What do you think, Jo?" Meg asked.

"You look well enough, I suppose," said Jo.

"Well enough?" Meg repeated.

"It's just a silly piece of lace," Jo said. "Not the crown jewels. I don't see what all the fuss is about."

"Jo's jealous," Amy said. "Aren't you, Jo?"

"No," Jo said, but Meg could see the storm clouds in Jo's eyes. When her sister got that look, it could only mean trouble.

"Jo, dear, what is bothering you?" Marmee asked.

"It's not fair!" Jo shouted. "Why should Aunt March bring Meg something from Europe and nothing for Beth or Amy?"

"Or for you, you mean," Amy said.

"Don't you mind?" Jo asked. "Don't you see how unfair it is?"

"No," Amy said. "Aunt March loves me, and someday she'll bring me a gift every bit as wonderful as the lace she's given Meg."

"Then what of Beth?" Jo asked. "Doesn't she count?"

"I don't mind that Aunt March didn't give me anything," said Beth. "I'm glad, really. If she had, I'd have to thank her again and again.

15

And Aunt March always makes me so nervous. If she doesn't think about me, I don't have to think about her."

"Then she should have brought me something!" Jo cried. "Meg only got the lace because she's the oldest. And that's not fair!"

"What's not fair?" Father asked, coming through the door. "What are my little women so concerned about?"

"Father!" cried Jo, throwing herself into her father's embrace. "Father, Aunt March brought Meg a present!"

"That was kind of her," Father replied. "Is it that lace I see so fetchingly draped upon Meg's head?"

"It is, Father," Meg said, removing the lace and folding it into a square. "Would you like to see it?"

"Very much," said Father. Meg handed him the lace and watched as he examined it. "It's beautiful," he said. "And it looked lovely on you, Meg."

"It's so big," Jo said. "I think Meg should cut it into four pieces and share it with us."

"Oh, no," said Marmee. "Jo, that simply wouldn't do."

"But it's not fair otherwise," Jo said. "Why should Meg be the only one to get a gift? She doesn't love Aunt March. She isn't even interested in her stories. All she wanted to do was laugh at her."

"I wasn't laughing at Aunt March," Meg said. "I was laughing at myself. And I love Aunt March every bit as much as you do."

"Now, girls," Father said. "We all agree Aunt March can be difficult at times. But that doesn't mean we love her any the less. There are other people in this room who are on occasion difficult, and that doesn't diminish our love for them, now, does it?"

"I'm sorry, Father," Beth said. "I try not to be difficult, but sometimes it just comes over me."

Father laughed. "You weren't the one I was thinking of, Bethy," he said. "But you're right. Being difficult does come over all of us on occasion. Doesn't it, Jo?"

"I'm not being difficult," Jo said. "I'm noting an injustice. You always tell us to be aware of injustices, Father, and to speak up against them."

Father looked directly at Jo. "It was not unjust of Aunt March to bring a present to Meg," he said. "She saw the lace, she thought of Meg, and she was generous enough to purchase it for her. You know perfectly well what I mean by injustice, Jo, and a present for one of your sisters is not what I mean."

"You don't love me!" Jo cried. "Nobody does! Nobody ever will in this family!" With that, she ran all the way up to her private retreat in the attic.

Meg looked at the lace. "I'm sorry," she said.

"You have nothing to apologize for," Father said. "Jo must learn she cannot always have everything her way. It's a lesson we all have to learn over and over again."

Meg nodded. Someday she'd marry, wearing her beautiful lace. She only hoped her husband, whoever he might be, would have less of a temper than her younger sister.

"Jo will be down by suppertime," Amy predicted, and she was right. Just as Hannah announced that supper was ready, Jo joined her family.

"I'm sorry," she said. "I shouldn't have carried on so."

"I knew you wouldn't stay angry for long," Beth said. "You're too good a person, Jo. I knew you'd be happy for Meg and her good fortune."

Jo nodded.

"I'm glad that's all settled," Marmee said. "Come, girls. Let's not keep Hannah and her fine food waiting."

19

During supper, Marmee repeated many of Aunt March's stories to Father. Her retellings left out all the dull parts, and everyone laughed at the funnier incidents.

"I must call on Aunt March tomorrow," Father said, "and hear her versions of these stories. I suspect they won't be quite so entertaining."

"I'm only telling you what she told us," Marmee protested. "Although it's possible I'm leaving out some of the details."

"And making the stories all the better for your editing," Father said. "Listen, Jo, and learn. What is left out of a story can be quite as effective as what is put in."

"Pardon me?" Jo said, and as soon as she did, Meg's heart sank. Jo was with them in body, but her mind was clearly elsewhere, and Meg knew where.

"Perhaps my retelling wasn't so interesting," Marmee said. "Jo, help Hannah with the dishes."

Jo scowled, but she got up and carried the dishes to the kitchen.

"Meg, don't worry about Jo," Marmee said. "She gets into these moods, but they never last for long."

"I can't cut the lace up," Meg said. "I just can't, Marmee."

"Of course not," Marmee agreed. "Why don't I put it away someplace for safekeeping? If the lace isn't around for Jo to notice, I'm sure she'll forget all about it."

"Must we?" Meg asked. "I love the lace so much, Marmee. You know I'll be careful with it. I'm not ready for you to put it away. I want a chance to look at it some more."

"Oh, dear," Marmee said. "I don't know what is best."

"Jo must learn that what belongs to Meg belongs to Meg," Father said. "We all agree Meg will be careful with the lace. I do suggest, though, that when you no longer feel the desire to look at the lace, Meg, you give it up for safekeeping. But until then, by all means keep it in your room."

"What if Jo wants to play with it?" Meg asked.

"It's your lace," Father said. "If you want Jo to play with it, then let her. But keep in mind, Aunt March gave you that lace for you to wear on your wedding day, and you should respect her wishes as well."

"That's what I want it for, Father," Meg said. "Thank you."

"May I see the lace again?" Amy asked. "I promise I won't touch it, Meg."

"I'd love to see it as well," Beth said.

"Wash your hands first," Meg ordered. "I'll wash mine also. We should all be clean when we touch it."

"Cleanliness is always a good idea," Father said. "Girls, you are all excused, so that you might wash your hands and examine this remarkable piece of lace."

The girls thanked their father and ran upstairs to their bedrooms, where they kept pitchers of water and washbasins.

In the room she shared with Jo, Meg carefully examined her sisters' hands. When she was sure there wasn't a speck of food or dirt on any of them, she removed the lace from its package and spread it out on her lap.

"It's so pretty," Beth said with a contented sigh.

"I wonder how much it cost," Amy said.

"Amy!" Meg said sharply. "We should never be concerned with how much a gift costs."

"I don't see why not," Amy replied.

"Because it's bad manners," Meg said. "A gift has just as much meaning if it costs pennies as it does if it costs dollars."

"I prefer the dollar gifts," Amy said. "When my duke courts me, he'll give me diamonds and emeralds."

"I don't need diamonds and emeralds," Meg said. "But I do love this lace."

"It isn't right to love things," Jo said, entering the room. "It's people you should love, Meg."

"But *I* love things!" Beth cried. "I love my dollies, even though I don't think of them as things. I love my piano. And I love our home. Am I wrong to love so many things?"

Meg knew how much Jo loved Beth. She held her breath to see how Jo would respond.

"I misspoke," Jo said slowly. "Of course there are things we love. I love sunsets and full moons and the look of a clean piece of paper on my desk. Those are good things to love, just as your dolls and piano and our home are good things to love."

"When my duke gives me diamonds and emeralds, I'll love them a lot," Amy announced.

"I'm sure you will," Jo said. "But diamonds are bad things to love. Just as that piece of lace is a bad thing to love."

"What are you saying?" Meg asked. "That only the things you and Beth love are good? That the things Amy and I might love are bad?"

"Jo didn't mean that," Beth said. "Did you, Jo?"

"Of course not," Jo said. "What I meant was . . ." But she was silent, as though trying to think of what it was she did mean.

"I don't care what Jo means," Amy said.

"I'm going to love everything my duke gives me. And if I don't want to share my diamonds and emeralds with Jo, then I won't."

"I'm not asking for your diamonds and emeralds, you silly goose," Jo said. "They don't exist and they never will."

"I am not a silly goose!" Amy cried. "You're mean, Jo. You're mean and jealous and rude!"

"And you're a greedy little pig," Jo said. "You and your silly duke. As though any duke would look at a girl like you."

"Jo," Meg said. "Stop it!"

"Who are you to give me orders?" Jo asked. "Oh, I'm sorry. I forgot. You're Aunt March's favorite. You're the one she brings splendid gifts to. You can say whatever you want because Aunt March loves you so."

"Maybe Aunt March does love me," Meg said. "Because I'm polite to her and because she knows I want to be a true lady. That's important to us, even if you don't think it matters."

"You were hardly even listening to her this afternoon," Jo said. "Some lady you are, when you could barely keep from laughing at her. I was the one who was interested in her stories. I was the one who sat by her feet and begged her to tell us about everything she saw. But she didn't care. You're her pet, and you're the one she gave the lace to."

"I'm not Aunt March's pet," Meg said. If anyone was, it was Amy, but Meg couldn't see any point in mentioning that. "I'm the oldest, that's all. On her next trip, perhaps Aunt March will bring you something, Jo. Or something for Beth or Amy. This trip, she thought of me. She gave me some lace for my wedding day. I don't see why you keep making such a fuss over it. It's not as if you want lace or anything else so delicate and fine."

"I want my share," Jo said. "If you loved me, you'd happily give me a fourth of that lace so that I might have something delicate and fine to call my own."

"No," Meg said. "I'm not going to, and that's that. And if you insist on spoiling things for me, Jo, then I'll just put the lace away and not look at it until you become a reasonable human being again."

"I'm the one who's reasonable," Jo grumbled. "It's you and Aunt March who aren't."

Meg frowned as she folded the lace and put it back in its wrapping. Someday, she told herself, she'd be able to enjoy the lace as much as it deserved.

Because Meg was a year older than Jo, she knew there had been a year in her life when the two sisters hadn't shared a bedroom. But they had for as long as Meg could remember. And for as long as she could remember, she had hated it when Jo went to bed angry.

That night was no exception. Jo put on her nightdress without saying a word to Meg. It didn't help that Meg was uncertain where to put the lace. She knew Jo wouldn't do anything to it, wouldn't slice it into pieces in the middle of the night, or hide it from her, or do anything except glower at it, but Meg still felt

28

the need to protect it from all the things she knew Jo would never do.

Meg tried to laugh at herself. It was hard to believe how joyous she'd felt that afternoon, even with Aunt March's visit looming. And then, after having received such a wonderful gift, she'd felt positively blessed.

It was unfair of Jo to make her feel so bad on such a good day. As she put on her night-dress, Meg considered how to protect the lace from such an angry, jealous younger sister.

She took the package and slipped it under her covers.

"Are you hiding the lace from me?" Jo asked. It was the first thing she had said to Meg in hours.

"I'll just sleep better knowing it's in my bed," Meg said, feeling like a fool even as she said it.

Jo must have thought Meg a fool as well, because she snorted. "Don't wrinkle it in your sleep," she said.

Meg hadn't thought of that. Even in its wrapping, the lace might be damaged if she rolled over on it or kicked it. She dug the package out and placed it under her pillow.

"That's much better," Jo said. "No robbers will ever think to look there."

"I'm not worried about robbers," Meg said. "Just nasty little sleepwalkers."

"I don't walk in my sleep!" Jo said.

"Fine," Meg said. "Then I don't have to worry about you. Good night, Jo."

"Good night to you, too," Jo said, making it sound like a terrible curse. She turned her back to Meg, which was her signal that all conversation was ended for the day.

Meg felt under the pillow for the package. She was afraid the weight of her head might crush the lace, but she couldn't think of any-place else to put it for the night.

If the lace got wrinkled, it would be Jo's fault, and that made Meg even angrier. She was used to Jo's tempers. But Meg couldn't remember a time when she had felt as much anger as she did now. Usually Jo's moods just made her sad or worried or a little frightened. But she no longer felt sad or worried about

Jo, and her fear had been lessened by the knowledge that the lace was safely under her head. Instead she felt anger, deep anger, because Jo had spoiled her gift with her selfish words.

"You should be ashamed of yourself," she said.

"I should be ashamed!" Jo cried, turning over angrily. "I'm not the one refusing to share my good fortune with my sisters."

"And I'm not the one scowling and fretting and behaving like a little spoiled brat," Meg replied. "You think just because you're angry, that means the whole world has to stop and take care of you."

"At least I don't need Aunt March to take care of me," Jo yelled. "I can do fine for myself."

"And why should Aunt March take care of an ungrateful wretch like you?" Meg shouted back. "You've never showed her or anyone else the least bit of courtesy."

"That's because I'm honest!" Jo screamed.

"Girls, girls," Marmee said, entering their

bedroom. "We could hear you all the way in the parlor."

"Oh, Marmee!" Meg cried. "Jo's being just terrible to me."

"I am not," Jo said. "She's the one who called me a spoiled brat."

"Because that's how you're behaving," Meg said. "Isn't she, Marmee?"

"You're both behaving like spoiled brats," Marmee said. "Meg, you're old enough to know how to behave."

"It's not my fault," Meg said. "She started it."

"I no longer care who started it," Marmee said. "There are other people in this family, and they don't need to be bothered by your ill tempers."

"I'm sorry, Marmee," Meg said. She waited for Jo to say the same, but Jo offered no such apology.

"I know you are, Meg, but the problem still remains," Marmee said. "I think for tonight the lace had best stay with me. Where did you put it?"

Meg pulled the package out from under her pillow. "Here it is," she whispered. "Hide it, Marmee, so no one can find it."

"I heard that," Jo said.

"Good," Meg said. "I'm glad you did."

"That's enough," Marmee said. "Don't make me feel ashamed that you're my daughters. I intend to speak to both of you in the morning. Now, can I trust the two of you to keep quiet and go to sleep?"

"That's what I was trying to do," Jo said. "Before Meg attacked me with her words."

"Only because you've been behaving so dreadfully," Meg said.

"That's enough," Marmee repeated. "Jo, get out of bed at once. I'll bring Amy here, and you can spend the night with Beth."

"Fine," said Jo. "I'd rather sleep on the attic floor than spend the night with Meg."

"You won't have to sleep on any floor," Marmee replied. "Now, keep quiet and follow me."

Meg watched as Marmee led Jo out of her room. She could hear sleepy murmurings from her sisters' bedroom and soon saw Amy being half led, half carried to Jo's bed.

"Don't keep her up," Marmee said to Meg. "There's no reason for Amy to lose any more sleep because of the two of you."

"I'll be quiet, I promise," Meg whispered. She watched as Marmee gently laid Amy in Jo's bed, then bent down to kiss her youngest good night.

Meg held her breath, fearing that Marmee might not kiss her. To her relief, Marmee gave her a good-night kiss as well.

"Sleep tight," Marmee murmured. "And when you wake up, do try to return to your sweet self."

"I'll try," Meg promised. She only wished she could be sure Jo would return to her occasionally sweet self too.

CHAPTER 5

"Meg, Jo, I want to speak to both of you after you've finished your breakfast," Marmee said the next morning.

"Yes, Marmee," the girls replied.

Meg began eating a little faster. Whatever Marmee had to say, she wanted to have it done with. Besides, she didn't want to be late to school.

Jo always ate quickly. Meg raced to keep pace with her. She was aware of Beth and Amy's curious eyes, but neither she nor Jo made any effort to speak to them.

"I'm done," Jo said, as though she'd accomplished a great feat.

"I'm through as well," Meg said. The girls got up and walked toward the parlor. Usually they'd be hand in hand, or running and laughing together. This morning they barely walked side by side.

"Girls," Marmee said, gesturing for them to sit down. Meg chose one chair, Jo another.

"Your father and I are very disturbed by your behavior," Marmee began. "It concerns us, Meg, that you might think a possession is more important than one of your sisters."

"I don't feel that way," Meg protested.

Jo humphed.

"Silence, Jo," Marmee said. "You'll have your turn soon enough."

"I was pleased Aunt March gave me the lace," Meg said. "I was more than happy to let Jo and Beth and Amy admire it also, Marmee. Everything would have been fine if Jo hadn't behaved so badly."

"We're not speaking about Jo," Marmee

said. "We're speaking about you, Meg. Now, what do you think you can do to restore peace in this family?"

"Why should I have to do anything?" Meg asked.

"Because you're a member of this family and I asked you a question," Marmee said. "That's why."

Meg couldn't ever remember hearing Marmee use that tone. She tried to think what she could offer that would satisfy Marmee. But the only thing she could come up with was the lace, and she had no intention of giving it to Jo.

"I'm sorry," she said. "Truly I am, Marmee. But this isn't my fault, and I don't know what to say."

"Do you love Jo?" Marmee asked.

Of course Meg did, but she was reluctant to admit it. She merely nodded.

"Very well," Marmee said. "Now, Jo, it's your turn. What do you have to say for yourself?"

"It's so unfair!" Jo cried. "All of it. All I

wanted was my fair share, and Meg's being horrible and selfish and I said absolutely nothing to her last night and she said the cruelest things to me. She called me names and yelled at me, and it's all because of that wretched piece of lace. She does love it more than she loves me. She loves it more than she loves anybody, Marmee, because she's selfish and mean and cruel."

"I am not!" Meg cried. "You're the one who's selfish and mean. Isn't she, Marmee?"

Marmee shook her head. "I don't know either of you," she said. "You're both behaving like strangers. Go to school, both of you. Perhaps by this afternoon you'll return as the loving sisters and daughters I've taken so much pride in."

"Don't you love us anymore?" Meg asked.

"Of course I love you," Marmee said. "But this morning I don't particularly *like* either of you. Now, go to school and leave me alone. I really don't care to spend any more time with you just now."

Meg and Jo left the parlor. They walked in

silence to their bedroom, gathered their books and their coats, then left the house.

Amy moved to Meg's side, and Beth walked by Jo. But the younger girls didn't chatter as they usually did.

Meg wondered if there was something she could say to make things better. She hated this angry silence, and she was sure Jo hated it as well.

"Jo," she said softly as they approached the school.

"I have nothing to say to you," Jo replied.

Amy clutched Meg's hand. "I love you," she said to Meg.

"I love you, too," Meg said. "And I love you also, Bethy."

Beth turned back to face Meg. "I know," she said. "And we love you also, Meg."

Meg felt better after that. Jo might not love her, and Marmee might be angry at her, but Amy and Beth still loved her, and that would have to be enough for now.

Meg forced herself to pay attention to

her teacher that morning. Soon she lost herself in her schoolwork. She noticed that Jo was also listening keenly to what their teacher had to say. Both girls were called on to answer questions, and both gave the correct responses. Meg was glad Jo got the right answer, because she feared that Jo might have held it against her if she'd answered wrongly.

Meg and Jo always ate lunch together, but that day Meg made no effort to join her younger sister, and Jo was equally cool to her. Instead Meg sat by her friend Mary Howe.

"I'm so glad you're having lunch with me," Mary said. "Mrs. March paid a call on my mother yesterday, and she told her she was bringing you a wonderful gift from Europe. But she wouldn't tell Mother what it was, and I've been so curious ever since. So please tell me, Meg, what is it?"

"It's a piece of Belgian lace," Meg said, and just seeing how eager Mary was for details made her rejoice in the present once again. "Oh, Mary, it's so beautiful. Aunt March said she bought it for me to wear at my wedding."

"How romantic," Mary said. "What a wonderful gift. Do you think I might see it?"

"Of course," Meg said. "Why don't you walk home with me after school today? Marmee is keeping it for me so that no harm will come to it, but I'm sure she'd be happy for you to see it."

"I'd love to," Mary replied. "Real Belgian lace. Aren't you lucky, Meg, that your aunt thought to bring you something so splendid?"

"Yes, I am," Meg said. "I'm very lucky." She glanced at Jo, who was sitting in a corner, eating her lunch in glowering silence.

"Is there something the matter with Jo?" Mary asked. "I spoke to her this morning, and she hardly seemed to acknowledge me."

Meg thought about telling Mary just how terrible Jo had become. But even though she knew Mary would take her side and agree with her that Jo was positively monstrous, she didn't care to let Mary know that there were any problems in the March household.

"Jo has a headache," she said instead, suspecting it wasn't even a lie. "She hasn't felt well since yesterday."

"She's jealous," Mary said. "I'm sure of it. My brother gets that way with me sometimes, when Father brings me a gift after he's been away."

"Then it's normal?" Meg asked.

Mary nodded. "Nasty, but normal," she said. "I must admit, sometimes I get jealous when Father brings Willie something and seems to forget about me."

Meg smiled gratefully at Mary. She was such a good friend, so understanding. "You and Willie don't stay angry long, do you?" she asked. "The jealousy doesn't last forever?"

"No, of course not," said Mary. "If you want, I'll talk to Jo for you."

"Not right now," Meg replied. "Perhaps after school."

"I'd be glad to," Mary said. "And I can't wait to see your lovely piece of lace."

"I can't wait to see it again myself," Meg said. Suddenly her lunch tasted better, and the afternoon was no longer something to dread.

Sisters were the best, Meg thought. But sometimes friends were even better.

CHAPTER 6

As close as Meg and Jo were, there were many days when they didn't walk home together. Both girls had other friends, and sometimes they had errands to run, or just desired a bit of privacy.

After the school bell rang, Meg gathered her belongings, located Beth and Amy in the school yard, and began the walk home with Mary by her side. Beth, who knew Mary but was shy, lagged behind. Amy chattered away merrily about the various dukes and earls Aunt March had encountered.

Meg had made no effort to include Jo and was not surprised to see her sister go off in a different direction. She would have felt better had she seen Jo accompanied by some of her friends, the many boys who accepted Jo as one of their own and allowed her to run and play with them. But Jo maintained her solitary mood and walked away from school alone.

"Jo will feel better soon," Mary assured Meg as the girls walked to the March house.

"I hope so," Meg said. She felt a sadness inside, replacing the anger of the morning. She couldn't remember ever feeling so apart from Jo, the sister she shared everything with.

"Jo gets into terrible tempers," Amy declared. "She yells and screams and sulks something fierce. Then the storm blows over and she's all sunshine again. That's when I love her the best."

"I love Jo all the time," Beth said quietly. "But she really can be difficult when she's angry."

"The duke I marry will have no temper at all," said Amy. "He'll smile all the time and cover me with diamonds."

She sounded so certain and so grand that

the other girls all laughed. Amy pouted, but then she laughed too.

"I shall remove the diamonds only when I bathe," she proclaimed, which made the girls laugh all the louder.

It felt good to be laughing. Meg only wished Jo were with them, enjoying their good humor and the early spring day. But Amy was right. When Jo got over her anger, she was like sunshine. And Meg had never known Jo's temper to last beyond a day or two.

Soon Jo would be herself again, and Meg would certainly do nothing more to provoke her. Marmee would like all her daughters again, and peace would return to the March household.

When that happened, Meg would allow Jo to look at the lace, even try it on (assuming her hands were freshly washed and Meg was there to supervise). And Jo would be welcome to wear the lace on her wedding day. Meg could even picture her younger sister, with her beautiful long hair, and the precious lace draped gracefully upon her head.

Meg laughed out loud.

"What's so funny?" Mary asked.

"Nothing," Meg said. "I was just thinking about all of us as brides."

"I don't think that's funny," said Amy. "I'm not sure I want you at my wedding, Meg, if you're going to laugh at me and the duke."

"Meg won't laugh at a duke," Beth said. "An earl maybe, but never a duke."

The girls laughed even harder.

Marmee met them at the door, a smile on her face. "I heard my little women laughing again," she said as she ushered them in. Then she noticed that the fourth girl wasn't Jo but Mary Howe instead.

"Where's Jo?" Marmee asked.

"She didn't walk home with us," Meg replied, and some of her good feeling evaporated. "But Mary is here."

"Hello, Mrs. March," Mary said, with a little curtsy. "Meg was kind enough to invite me for a brief visit."

"She'd very much like to see the lace," Meg

said, taking off her coat and helping Mary off with hers.

"The lace," Marmee said.

"It was my idea," Mary said. "Mrs. March paid a call on my mother yesterday and told her she had brought a lovely gift home for Meg. Naturally I was curious about it."

"Mary can see it, can't she, Marmee?" Meg asked. "I promise you we'll be careful."

"It's your lace," Marmee replied. "But I do suggest you handle it very carefully."

"We will, Mrs. March," Mary said. "I know how valuable Belgian lace can be. I won't even touch it, if that's what you prefer. I'll just let Meg show it to me."

Marmee smiled, and Meg felt relieved. Marmee knew how trustworthy Mary was.

"The lace is on Meg's bed," said Marmee. "I decided that since the lace belonged to Meg, it was hers to deal with."

"Oh, thank you, Marmee!" Meg exclaimed. "Come, Mary. Let me show it to you right away."

"May I see it again?" Amy asked.

"And me too?" Beth asked.

Meg thought about how crowded her little bedroom could be with four girls in it. Mary had a beautiful large bedroom all her own. "Later," she said, not wanting Mary to feel overwhelmed by little sisters. "Right now I just want Mary to see it."

"Marmee, make Meg show us the lace," Amy wheedled.

Marmee began to lose her pleasant smile. "It's Meg's lace," she said. "If Meg wants you to wait, then you must wait."

For a moment Amy looked as though she were going to have a tantrum of her own. But then she smiled. "All right," she said. "But when Meg comes to me for diamonds, I'll make her wait as well."

The girls burst out laughing again, and after a second Marmee joined them. Meg led Mary upstairs while Beth and Amy went into the kitchen for bread and jam.

"I love your house so," Mary said as the

girls walked up the staircase. "It's always full of fun. I wish my house were more like yours."

"And I wish mine were more like yours," Meg said. "I can't imagine how wonderful it must be to have your own room."

"Sometimes, when Mama and Papa are traveling, it's quite lonely," Mary replied. "I know Willie and the servants are nearby, but my room gets so dark, it makes me frightened and sad. I'm sure you never feel that way."

Meg thought about the previous night. She'd been far too angry to be frightened or sad. "You're right," she said. "There are always too many of us for me to feel frightened or sad."

"That's why I envy you your home," Mary said. "Not all the time, of course. But some nights, I think of you and Jo sharing this room, whispering and laughing in your beds, and I wish my family were more like yours."

Meg smiled. It was easy for Mary to feel that way because she had money and a room of her own and no sister who was refusing to

51

speak to her. But there was no point in ex-
plaining all that. Instead Meg opened the
package and showed Mary the lace.

"Oh, my. It's even more beautiful than I
imagined," Mary breathed. "You'll be the most
beautiful bride ever when you wear it, Meg."

"Do you truly think so?" Meg asked. She
touched the lace gently, thrilling once again to
its quiet perfection.

"May I try it on?" Mary asked. "I should
love to pretend it's my wedding veil."

Meg nodded. She knew she could trust
Mary, who draped the lace carefully upon her
head.

"How do I look?" Mary asked.

Meg smiled. "You look like a beautiful
bride," she replied. "One worthy of a duke."

Mary laughed. "Amy merits the duke," she
said. "I'll settle for a count." She touched the
lace again, then ever so gingerly removed it
from her head and handed it back to Meg.
"Thank you," she said. "It was kind of you to
let me see it."

Meg thought of all the treasures Mary

52

owned and felt real joy that she too had something worth treasuring. "You may see the lace again if you want," she said. "Not too often, of course, because soon I'll give it to Marmee for safekeeping. But from time to time, I'll be taking it out, and you're more than welcome to come over when I do."

"I should like that," Mary said. "I like to imagine what sort of bridal gown I'll wear. The lace makes the daydreams seem more real."

"That's just how I feel!" Meg exclaimed.

"I should be going," Mary said, looking at her watch, which was one of Mary's many possessions Meg had envied on occasion. "Mama doesn't like it if I walk home by myself after dark."

"I'll see you to the road," Meg said. The girls went downstairs and got Mary's coat and books. Mary paid her respects to Marmee, then left the house with Meg by her side.

"Here's Jo!" Mary said as she and Meg reached the road. "Jo, I've just seen the lace. It's so beautiful."

Jo merely nodded and walked on.

Mary shook her head. "Perhaps I shouldn't have mentioned it," she said. "I was hoping Jo had returned to her sunshine state."

"Not yet, it would seem," Meg replied.

"I'm sure she'll feel better once she's had something to eat," Mary said. "Willie can be a bear on an empty stomach." She gave Meg a quick kiss on the cheek, then waved good-bye and began her walk home.

Meg went back to the house. Jo was quite the bear herself, she thought. And she doubted that bread and jam would solve the problem.

CHAPTER 7

"Where's Jo?" Meg asked Marmee as she entered the parlor.

"She took some bread and jam and went up to your room," Marmee replied.

"Oh, no!" Meg cried. "The lace is still on my bed. She'll ruin it."

"I'm sure it will be all right," Marmee said, but Meg could see from the concerned look in her eyes that Marmee wasn't at all sure.

Meg ran up the stairs to her bedroom. Jo was standing over Meg's bed, nibbling away at her bread and jam.

"Get away from the lace!" Meg shrieked. "Do you hear me? Right now, Jo!"

"I'm not doing anything to it," Jo said. "I'm just looking."

"You'll drip jam on it," Meg said. "I know you, Jo. You make a mess of everything. Go to your side of the room this very minute."

Jo stared at Meg and then very slowly began the three-step walk to her own bed.

"Faster," Meg said. She wanted to grab the lace and hide it, but she couldn't figure out how.

"I'm walking as fast as I can," Jo said. "It was a long, hard day and I'm weak from hunger."

Usually when Jo said such humorous things, Meg laughed. But as long as the lace was in jeopardy, Meg felt no laughter inside her.

Jo sat down on her bed and continued to eat her snack. "Mary was allowed to look upon your most precious possession," she said. "How noble of you."

"She asked to see it," Meg said. "And I knew she'd be careful with it."

"So you actually let her touch it?" Jo asked.

56

Meg looked at her sister. Jo had jam on her cheek. "Of course I let her touch it," Meg replied. "Mary is a lady. She keeps herself clean. She would never damage something so fine. And she wasn't mean or jealous. She was happy for me that Aunt March brought me such a nice present."

"So I'm dirty and mean and jealous," Jo said. She angrily wiped the jam off her cheek.

"You said it, I didn't," said Meg. She couldn't believe how easy it was to feel rage at Jo again.

"You let some friend of yours play with your precious lace, but you won't even let your sister stay in the same room with it," Jo said.

"My other sisters are more than welcome to," Meg said. "And don't start yelling. I can't bear to have Marmee get that look on her face again."

"You're the one responsible for that look," Jo said. "With your selfishness and your nasty tongue."

"All I'm doing is protecting what is mine," Meg said.

"Why?" Jo asked. "What do you think I'll do to that precious piece of lace of yours?" She lunged toward the bed and grabbed the lace in her jam-smeared hands.

"Give that back to me!" Meg cried, seizing the lace.

But Jo didn't relinquish it. "Not until you say you'll share it," she demanded.

"I'll never agree to that," Meg said. She tugged at the lace, trying desperately to get it from Jo before it was dirtied even more.

Jo persisted in holding on. The harder Meg pulled, the stronger Jo's grasp became. Soon Meg didn't care what happened to the lace, just as long as it was hers to hold. Using all her strength, she pulled. Jo resisted with all her might. The girls fought in silent rage until Meg's anger gave her sufficient strength to pull the lace away from her sister.

But as she did, Meg heard a horrible tearing sound. Jo heard it as well and released the lace. It was too late. The piece of lace was ripped nearly in half.

"No!" Meg screamed. "You destroyed it!"

"You were the one who pulled!" Jo shouted back. "It's your fault."

"Mine!" Meg screeched. "I hate you, Jo! I hate you!"

"Girls!" Marmee shouted, racing up the stairs. "Stop it right now!"

Meg threw herself into Marmee's arms. "Jo destroyed my lace!" she cried. "See, Marmee. Jo tore it! I hate her!"

"Stop it," Marmee said. "Never say that, Meg. Never."

"But she tore it," Meg said, bursting into tears. "Jo ripped it and destroyed it."

"I did not," Jo muttered. "Meg did. She kept tugging at it, and it's all her fault."

"Jo, keep quiet," Marmee said. "Meg, let me look at the lace."

Meg handed the torn and jam-stained lace to her mother.

"Oh, dear," Marmee said. "Oh, girls, how could you?"

"Meg started it," Jo said. "Letting Mary play with it, and then acting so high and mighty with me."

"She was going to get jam all over it," Meg sobbed. "She did, too. See, Marmee. See that stain!"

"I see it," Marmee said. "And I see two sisters behaving like savage enemies. And I don't like anything I'm seeing."

Jo began to cry as well. Meg looked at her once-beautiful piece of lace and wept even harder.

"Oh, girls," Marmee said again. But before she had a chance to continue, there was a knock on the front door.

Meg heard Aunt March's booming voice as Beth opened the door and let her in.

"I thought I'd pay a call," Aunt March announced. "Is your mother at home, Beth?"

Marmee rolled her eyes. "Stay here," she whispered to Meg and Jo. "And don't say another word. Do you hear me?"

Meg and Jo both nodded tearfully.

"I'll see if I can get Aunt March to leave right away," Marmee whispered. "If I can't, and if you must come downstairs, don't tell her about the lace. I'll handle it my own way."

Meg was stunned. She had never imagined that Marmee could conspire in any way. But Meg and Jo both nodded again to show that they knew what was expected of them.

Marmee raced down the stairs. Meg glanced at Jo's sullen, tear-stained face. She wondered if she could ever find it in her heart to forgive her younger sister. And as she looked at the ruined lace, Meg seriously doubted it.

CHAPTER 8

*M*eg tiptoed to the staircase. Jo followed her. Neither of them said a word.

"I was paying a call nearby," Meg heard Aunt March say, "and I thought I would drop in and tell you some more of my little adventures abroad."

"How kind of you, Aunt March," Marmee said. "We'd love to hear them, but right now we're very busy preparing for supper. Of course you're more than welcome to eat with us, if you'd like."

Meg held her breath. Aunt March never ate

with them, preferring, as she did, the meals cooked for her at her own home.

"No, thank you," Aunt March responded, just as Meg had hoped. "And since you are busy, I won't stay but a minute."

"Thank you for understanding," Marmee said.

"I should like to see the girls," Aunt March said. "Margaret in particular. I paid a call on Mrs. Howe yesterday and told her I'd brought Margaret a special gift from Belgium. I'm curious to hear if Mrs. Howe made mention of it to her daughter."

Meg gave Jo a look of terror and despair. Jo shrugged. Meg wasn't sure how to interpret Jo's shrug, and felt anger surge in her again. Jo had destroyed her lace, and now Meg had to go downstairs and chat with Aunt March about it.

"Meg!" Marmee called, and Meg could hear the desperation in her mother's voice. "Aunt March is here, and she'd like to see you."

"Coming!" Meg replied, giving Jo one last look before walking down the stairs. She moved as slowly as she could, trying to will Aunt March to vanish. But the elderly woman was still standing in the hallway as Meg reached the first floor.

"Hello, Aunt March," Meg said, curtsying slightly. "How nice to see you so soon after your last call."

"I'm pleased to see you have manners," Aunt March responded. "Good manners are the mark of a true lady. Breeding is what counts most in the world, and that's most fortunate, since your parents have no wealth to bestow upon you."

"Yes, Aunt March," Meg said. "I try to be a lady at all times. Really I do."

"I'm sure you do, Margaret," Aunt March said. "I know this must be a short call, but I can't stand very much longer."

"Oh, I'm sorry, Aunt March," Marmee said. "Of course we can go into the parlor. Meg, go to the kitchen and tell Hannah supper will be delayed."

"Yes, Marmee," Meg said, delighted to have an excuse to leave the room. She walked as slowly as she could, and found Hannah by the stove, stirring the stewpot. Beth and Amy were sitting in the kitchen, enjoying the warmth of the room.

"Marmee says to tell you supper will be a little late tonight," Meg said. "Aunt March has dropped by unexpectedly."

"There's no rush with a stew," Hannah said. "Just let me know when Mrs. March has left, and I'll set the table."

"Thank you," Meg said. She looked around the kitchen for a job only she could do but couldn't find any. Reluctantly, she left the security of the kitchen for the terrors of the parlor.

"There you are," Aunt March said as Meg approached her. "Sit down, Margaret, and tell me if Mary Howe asked you about the gift I brought you."

"Yes, she did, Aunt March," Meg replied. "She was most curious about it."

"Heh, heh," Aunt March said. That was as close to a laugh as Meg had ever heard from her. "Mrs. Howe does put on airs. She's good enough, I suppose, as good as a woman can be who hails from Vermont. But she does think that since she married into the Howes, she's a true Bostonian. She goes on so about her travels, as though she were the only one ever to see Europe."

"I've always found Mrs. Howe to be very pleasant company," Marmee said. "Meg and Jo are quite fond of Mary and Willie."

"Josephine," Aunt March said. "Where is she? And Beth and Amy as well. Are they all hiding from me today?"

"No, of course not," Marmee said. "It's just that you called at such an unusual time, Aunt March. You never call this late in the afternoon."

"Europe does that to you," Aunt March replied. "It changes your outlook about so many things. What a shame you've never been abroad. I do hope someday your daughters will have the chance to see the world. Now, where are they?"

"Beth and Amy are in the kitchen," Meg said. "I'll go and get them." She was sure things would be easier if there were more of them in the room with Aunt March.

This time she walked rapidly. "Aunt March wants to see you," she whispered to her sisters. "Come with me."

"Must we?" Beth whispered back.

Meg nodded.

"I like Aunt March," Amy declared, and skipped toward the parlor to show just how much she did. Meg and Beth followed at a slower pace.

"Now, tell me, Margaret," Aunt March said. "You said Mary Howe was curious when you told her about the lace. Did she have any other reaction?"

"She was very happy for me," Meg said, wishing she could change the subject.

"Happy for you," Aunt March said. "Didn't she want to see the lace?"

"Yes, she did," Meg said. "Of course she did. She came here after school so she could admire it."

Aunt March nodded. "I trust she was properly impressed."

"She was," Meg said. "Mary claimed it was even more beautiful than she'd imagined."

"Pretty words," Aunt March said. "I trust you showed great care with the lace."

"Of course, Aunt March," Meg replied.

"Meg has spoken of little besides the lace since you gave it to her," Marmee said. "I've never seen a gift have so much of an effect on any of my daughters."

"Heh, heh," Aunt March cackled. "Beth, Amy, has Meg allowed you to admire her lace?"

"Oh, yes, Aunt March," Amy said. "It's the most beautiful thing I've ever seen."

"Someday perhaps I'll purchase something similar for you," Aunt March said. "And for you as well, Beth."

"Thank you, Aunt March," Beth and Amy said.

"I might even get something nice for Josephine," said Aunt March. "Where is that girl, anyway? Probably in the attic, writing another of her wild tales. She'll ruin her eyes doing all that writing, and her eyes are one of her better features."

"I'll go and get her," Beth volunteered.

"No, I'll go," Amy said. "I left some of my things in her room last night, and I might as well fetch them now."

"Amy," Meg said, but since she had no other way of warning her about her recent argument with Jo, or about the state of the lace, she couldn't finish her sentence. Marmee also gave a look of despair, but Amy was oblivious to their concern and scurried from the parlor.

Jo came down the stairs shortly after Amy had left. "Hello, Aunt March," she said.

"Josephine," Aunt March said. "We were just talking about the lace I gave Margaret. Have you admired it?"

Jo nodded.

"I should imagine so," Aunt March said. "Such a beautiful piece of lace. I looked at many different patterns before selecting that one, you know."

"How very thoughtful of you," Marmee

said. But before they had a chance to continue with the discussion, Amy came running down the stairs.

"Oh, Marmee!" she cried. "Something terrible has happened to Meg's lace. It's all torn and stained!"

"What?" Aunt March said, rising from the chair and pointing her walking stick at Meg. "Margaret, what have you done to my lace?"

CHAPTER 9

*M*eg suddenly thought of a dream she'd once had, in which Aunt March had pointed her walking stick at the house and the house had burst into flames. In spite of herself, she looked around to see if the March home was indeed on fire. She almost regretted the fact that it wasn't.

"There was an accident, Aunt March," Marmee said. "Naturally we were going to tell you."

"Was this Mary Howe's doing?" Aunt March asked.

"Mary had nothing to do with it," Meg said. She paused, just in case the house decided to start burning. When it didn't, she knew she would have to take responsibility. "It was my fault, Aunt March. I was careless with the lace and I damaged it."

"Damaged it?" Aunt March said. "From the sound of it, you ruined it."

Meg looked down at the floor. This moment, which she had known would come, was even worse than she had imagined.

"Amy, fetch me the lace," Aunt March said. "I want to see just what Meg has done to my present."

"Yes, Aunt March," Amy said.

They sat in silence until Amy returned with the lace. When Meg saw it, she nearly burst into tears again. The damage was even worse than she remembered.

"Ripped and stained," Aunt March said, handling the lace as though it were diseased. "Really, Margaret. I thought I could trust you with such a gift. How could you have been so careless?"

"I don't know," Meg said, trying hard not to cry. "It just happened."

73

"No, it didn't," Jo said.

Meg turned to face her sister. What did Jo plan to do now?

"It was my fault," Jo said. "All my fault."

"No, it wasn't," Meg said. "I was responsible too."

Jo shook her head. "Meg was trying to protect the lace. I went up to the bedroom eating a piece of bread and jam, and Meg was worried I'd get jam on the lace. We got into a fight over it, and I pulled at the lace and it ripped and I got jam on it as well. I ruined it, and I'm terribly, terribly sorry."

"It was my fault as well," Meg said. "I should have just let Jo look at it. I've been fighting with her since yesterday, and I've been horrible to her."

"I'm afraid the fault is mine," Marmee said. "The girls were so difficult, and I simply didn't know how to handle them. I let things get out of hand."

"It was my fault too," Beth said.

They all looked at her.

"Well, it was," she said. "Usually I can talk

to Jo and make her laugh, but yesterday and today, she was so angry, she scared me."

"I scared you?" Jo asked. "Oh, Bethy, I'm sorry."

"It sounds as though you are all sorry," Aunt March said.

Marmee smiled sadly. "I told you I'd never seen a gift have such an effect on my girls," she said.

"You girls fought over the lace?" Aunt March asked. "Josephine, was it the lace that put you in such a fierce temper?"

"Yes, Aunt March," Jo replied. "I was jealous that Meg had gotten such a lovely gift and I hadn't."

Aunt March harrumphed. "Then I suppose to some extent it was my fault as well," she said.

"Your fault, Aunt March?" Amy asked. "I thought you and I were the only ones who didn't ruin the lace."

"Heh, heh, heh," Aunt March said. "I'm afraid, little Amy, you are the only one without blame."

"It wasn't your fault, Aunt March," Marmee said. "It was a lovely gift."

"But I didn't think of the other girls," Aunt March said. "Naturally, if you give one thing to one girl, all the others will want something as well. That's simply human nature. No matter how fine our breeding."

"Still, I behaved terribly," Jo said.

"So did I," said Meg.

"And the lace suffered for it," Aunt March said. She examined it more carefully, holding it to the window as the setting sun beamed a last shard of light.

"We might still be able to mend it," Marmee said. "And perhaps the stain will come out if we wash it often enough. After all, Meg won't be getting married for quite a few years."

"My dear, this lace is beyond redemption," Aunt March said. "It should never see the light of day again."

"I'm so sorry," Jo said. "The lace never would have been ruined if I'd behaved myself. I'll pay you back. I don't know how, but I will, I promise."

"A fine offer on your part," Aunt March said. "But perhaps a more practical solution would be to take the lace to a seamstress and have her create an undergarment for Margaret to wear on her wedding day."

"Why, Aunt March!" Meg exclaimed. She never thought she'd hear Aunt March say anything as daring as "undergarment."

"A girl should feel pretty all over on her wedding day," Aunt March said. She looked at the shocked faces that surrounded her. "Heh, heh, heh, heh," she cackled. "Heh, heh, heh!"

CHAPTER 10

*B*eth and Amy went to bed early that night, exhausted from all the events and strain of the late afternoon. Meg was tired as well, but she knew there were still things to be said to Jo and to Marmee.

Father went to his study after supper, to work on his Sunday sermon. Marmee picked up her mending and sat in the parlor by the fire. Meg sat by her side, and soon Jo joined them.

"I was upstairs," Jo said. "Apologizing to Beth and Amy."

"Amy must have liked that," Meg said.

Jo shrugged. "It was Bethy I really needed

to apologize to," she said. "But I didn't want to slight Amy, so I included her as well. She seemed more than happy to forgive me. She even said something about some duke forgiving me, whatever that means."

Meg laughed. "She has it in her head that she'll marry a duke someday," she said. "He's going to shower her with diamonds."

"Better diamonds than lace," Jo said. "Meg, I really don't know what got into me. It was as if some demon took control and made me act the way I did. Can you ever forgive me?"

"Only if you forgive me," Meg said. "And you too, Marmee. You were both right. I really did love the lace more than I loved my sister."

Marmee put down her mending. "Your father and I try to give you all we can," she said. "We decided a long time ago that leading a good life was more important than making money. We know there are people who believe you can do both, but we were glad to sacrifice any chance at material wealth for spiritual riches."

"But that's the right thing to do," Meg said. "Everyone knows that."

Marmee smiled. "Not everyone," she said. "Sometimes even I have my doubts. I'll see something pretty and want it for myself or for one of my daughters. Or I'll think how much easier it would be if we could afford a horse and carriage of our own. All of us want more than we have. If we didn't, there would be no progress. In my lifetime, I've seen the coming of trains and telegraphs. Who knows how many new inventions there'll be for you girls to witness?"

"Then it's good to want more?" Meg asked.

"I don't know that I'd say good," Marmee said. "But as Aunt March put it, it's human nature."

"It's not human nature for me to be so angry," Jo said. "So jealous and mean."

"It's very human," Marmee said. "Not good, but human."

"But I was wrong too," Meg said. "All I could think of was the lace. I didn't once think about how Jo must be feeling."

Marmee nodded. "Perhaps you girls haven't had enough gifts in your lives. Perhaps that's why this one took on such importance."

"Oh, no," Meg said. "I've had everything I've ever needed."

"We all have," Jo said. "Much more than we need."

"Needs and wants are not necessarily the same thing," Marmee replied. "A person can be full at the end of a meal and still want to eat dessert."

"Dessert is fine," Jo said. "Just as long as it's not jam and bread."

Meg and Marmee both laughed.

"It feels good to be able to laugh," Meg said. "There were times last night and today I thought I might never laugh with you again, Jo."

"I thought I would never laugh myself," Jo replied. "Marmee, why do I behave that way?"

"You have my temper, dear," Marmee said. "I've worked my whole life to control it, but it's a battle still. I was so angry at the two of you today, I didn't know how to deal with you. And that's one reason why the lace was destroyed."

"I'm glad it was," Meg said. "It's what I deserved to have happen. I said I hated Jo, and I never should have said that."

"We say things in anger we regret later," Marmee said. "Sometimes we regret them for the rest of our lives. At least you girls have had a chance to make up and realize how much you love each other."

"More than I could love any piece of lace," Meg said. "Or even one of those diamonds the duke keeps promising Amy."

This time Jo laughed as well.

"Sometimes we have to taste the bitter to truly appreciate the sweet," Marmee said. "But I still would have preferred not to endure the past twenty-four hours."

"I'm sorry, Marmee," Meg said. "I'll never behave that badly again."

"Nor will I," Jo said. "Although this beastly temper of mine probably won't go away overnight."

"Probably not," Marmee said. "I know mine hasn't."

"One good thing did happen because of all of this," Meg said. "We actually got to hear Aunt March mention undergarments."

Marmee smiled. "Aunt March was quite gracious, really. I want both of you girls to write her notes of apology tomorrow."

"I will," Meg promised.

"I will also," Jo said. "Although I'm not sure I'll ever be able to look at her without thinking about *her* undergarments."

"Jo!" Meg exclaimed.

"Just joking," Jo said. "Heh, heh, heh, heh, heh."

She sounded so much like Aunt March that Marmee and Meg roared with laughter. As Jo joined them, Meg looked at her mother and her sister and knew that her family was the greatest gift of all.

PORTRAITS OF LITTLE WOMEN ACTIVITIES

SCALLOPED APPLES

The aromatic blend of apples and spices makes this dessert one that is sure to be devoured.

INGREDIENTS
½ cup white sugar
¼ teaspoon ground cinnamon
¼ teaspoon ground nutmeg
¼ teaspoon ground cloves
4 medium tart apples, peeled, cored, and thinly sliced
½ cup butter or margarine

2 cups fresh, unseasoned bread crumbs (about 4
   slices of stale bread, any type)

Preheat oven to 350 degrees.

1. Blend the sugar and spices in a bowl.
2. Toss the thinly sliced apples into the sugar
   and spice mixture.
3. In a skillet, melt the butter slowly over
   medium heat, then add the bread crumbs,
   stirring and toasting lightly.
4. In a greased 8-inch square baking pan, layer
   half the apples, then half the crumbs, then
   add a second layer of apples and top with the
   remaining crumbs.
5. Bake about 45 minutes, or until the apples
   are tender.

Serve warm with a bit of vanilla ice cream or
sweetened whipped cream.

L A C E
B A R R E T T E

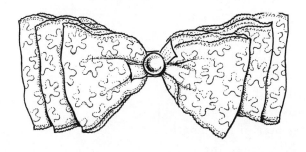

*This lovely hair adornment is perfect for
special occasions.*

MATERIALS

1 yard of 2-inch-wide white lace

6 inches of ½-inch-wide white double-sided satin
  ribbon

1 bottle of all-purpose clear glue

1 2½- or 3-inch metal barrette (from a craft
  store)

3 small white pearls

1. Cut the lace into
   three separate
   lengths: a 12-inch

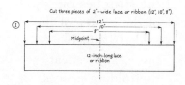

Cut three pieces of 2"-wide lace or ribbon (12", 10", 8").

①

12-inch-long lace
or ribbon

89

length, a 10-inch length, and an 8-inch length.

2. Take the 12-inch length of lace and fold the left side over the top with half of the cut edge overlapping the center of the length. Next, take the right side and fold it over so that half of the cut side overlaps the center and the left side. This should give you two loops, each about 5½ inches long.

3. Take the 10-inch piece of lace and lay it down carefully so that the center of the strip lies on top of the center of the folded 12-inch piece, and repeat the folding process.

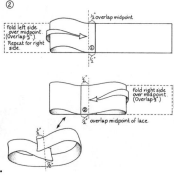

② ½ overlap midpoint

fold left side over midpoint. (Overlap ½") Repeat for right side.

① ½"

fold right side over midpoint (Overlap ½")

② ½" overlap midpoint of lace

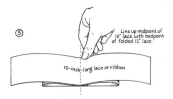

③ Line up midpoint of 10" lace with midpoint of folded 12" lace

10-inch-long lace or ribbon

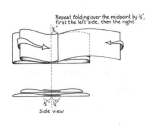

Repeat folding over the midpoint by ½", first the left side, then the right.

Side view

This will give you
two more loops,
each about 4½
inches long. You
should have two
loops on each side.

4. Lay the center of
the 8-inch piece of
lace on top of the
center of the
10-inch piece and
repeat the folding
process. You now
have another pair of
loops, each about
3½ inches long. You
should have three
loops on each side.

5. Take the length of
satin ribbon and
guide it under all
three pieces of lace,
stopping when you
have reached the
center of the lace
strips. Draw the
two pieces of ribbon
together, make a

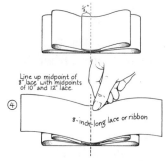

Line up midpoint of
8" lace with midpoints
of 10" and 12" lace.

④

8-inch-long lace or ribbon

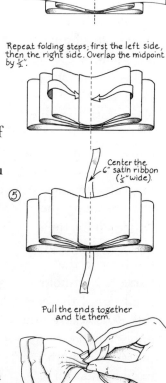

Repeat folding steps; first the left side,
then the right side. Overlap the midpoint
by ½".

⑤

Center the
6" satin ribbon
(½" wide).

Pull the ends together
and tie them.

loop, and tie it so
that all three pieces
of lace are gathered
into a bow shape.
Pull tightly. Cut the
ribbon's ends,
leaving ½ inch on
each side. Place a
small dab of glue at
the point of the tie
to keep it in place.
Hold the tie in
place until the glue
dries.

Pull the tie ends tight and place

a dab of glue here
to seal the tie.
Trim tie ends to ½" long.

6. Place a bead of glue
along the outside of
the barrette and
another along the
underside of the
lace bow. Fasten
the bow to the
barrette and hold
firmly until the glue
sets. Make sure you
apply equal
pressure to both
ends so that all
corners of the fabric

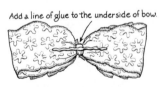

Apply line of glue to back of

the barrette...

Add a line of glue to the underside of bow.

stay in place. Allow
to dry thoroughly.
(To be sure you
apply solid pressure,
consider holding the
bow to the barrette
with several
clothespins.)

Press the bow to the barrette and
hold firmly till glue sets.

7. Place a dab of glue
on one of the pearls
(or other decoration
of your choice) and
fasten the pearl to
the center of the
bow where you've
tied off the ribbon.

Apply dab of glue
to pearl

⑦

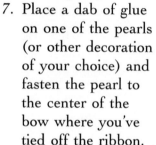

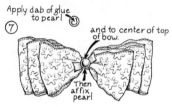

and to center of top
of bow.

Then
affix
pearl

Don't hesitate to use satin, patterned fabric,
or velour to decorate other barrettes. The more
you make, the more you'll have to choose from.

ABOUT THE AUTHOR OF
PORTRAITS OF LITTLE WOMEN

SUSAN BETH PFEFFER is the author of both middle-grade and young adult fiction. Her middle-grade novels include *Nobody's Daughter* and its companion, *Justice for Emily*. Her highly praised *The Year Without Michael* is an ALA Best Book for Young Adults, an ALA YALSA Best of the Best, and a *Publishers Weekly* Best Book of the Year. Her novels for young adults include *Twice Taken*, *Most Precious Blood*, *About David*, and *Family of Strangers*. Susan Beth Pfeffer lives in the town of Walkill, New York.

A WORD ABOUT
LOUISA MAY ALCOTT

LOUISA MAY ALCOTT was born in 1832 in Germantown, Pennsylvania, and grew up in the Boston-Concord area of Massachusetts. She received her early education from her father, Bronson Alcott, a renowned educator and writer, who eventually left teaching to study philosophy. To supplement the family income, Louisa worked as a teacher, a household servant, and a seamstress, and she wrote stories as well as poems for newspapers and magazines. In 1868 she published the first volume of *Little Women*, a novel about four sisters growing up in a small New England town during the Civil War. The immediate success of *Little Women* made Louisa May Alcott a celebrated writer, and the novel remains one of today's best-loved books. Alcott wrote until her death in 1888.